D1503828

Growing Pains & Petals

WRITTEN BY: OLIVIA CAFONE & LAUREN GOLDMAN
ILLUSTRATED BY: OLIVIA CAFONE

Text Copyright © 2021 by Olivia Cafone & Lauren Goldman
Illustrations Copyright © 2021 by Olivia Cafone

All rights reserved. No part of this publication may be reproduced or transmitted in any form or by any means, electronic, or mechanical, including photography, recording, or any information storage and retrieval system, without permission in writing from the publisher.

ISBN: 9798738815485

FOR ANY FLOWER,
BIG OR SMALL,
GREEN OR BLUE, WHO
NEEDS THE
REMINDER TO BE
PATIENT WHILE YOUR
PETALS GROW FOR
YOU.

It was a rainy day in Colorful Colorado.

The rain searched for the new flower buds to give them their first rain drop. Miss Daffodil rose from her sleep with glee and prepared to welcome the new baby buds in town.

As the raindrops fell, the baby buds sat ready to eat their first rain drop.

The drops fell onto their plates one by one. The baby buds were ready for their first taste of Colorful Colorado.

Miss Daffodil tended to the baby buds. She made sure each one had plenty to eat. She noticed one bud in the middle of the bunch. Violet was her name.

Violet hadn't taken a bite yet. Instead. she waited patiently for one of each color to reach her plate. When Violet had the whole rainbow, she pushed the colors together making beautiful new colors. The baby bud had colors all over her hands, and Miss Daffodil smiled.

It was another beautiful day at Greenhouse Elementary. The buds and Miss Rose spent a playful morning exploring the greenhouse, and they worked up quite an appetite.

"Okay my Kinderbuds! Grab your lunch boxes, it's time to eat." said Miss Rose.

As if she had a secret. Violet slowly opened her lunch box to see the colors she carefully collected that morning.

Curious eyes quickly turned to Violet's colorful plate.

"Look at all of those colors," said Jade. "Where did you get them?"

Violet grins. She is happy to share her special way of collecting rain drops.

Some attended art class with Miss Daffodil where they painted portraits and created clay sculptures.

It was summertime in Colorful Colorado. The sun was hot, and the smiles were big. The flowers and buds spent the summer swimming in their pools.

At the end of each day, the buds and flowers sang their favorite songs and enjoyed the summertime breeze.

Violet was so excited for the first day of school to show her friends what she spent the summer working on with Miss Daffodil.

She now knows how to turn her colorful plate of raindrops into art!

Violet waved to Olive and Jade. Before she could even say hello, she overheard them talking...

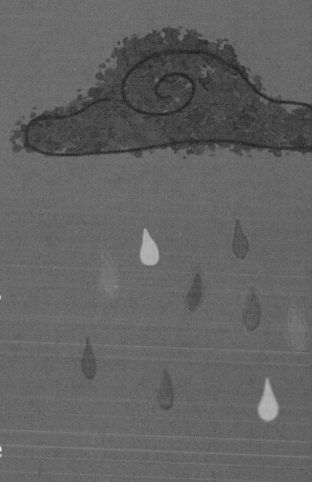

"Thanks! I got my third petal last night," said Jade. "Lucky! I only have one petal," Olive said with a frown.

Violet's smile dropped. She didn't have any petals yet. She was just a little green bud.

Violet hadn't even thought
about when she would see
her first petal.

It felt as if Violet had all eyes
on her, but not in the way she
was used to.

During art class, Violet was quiet. Miss Daffodil calmly knelt beside her. She could tell Violet was feeling blue.

"Why don't I have my petals yet? I'm still only a green bud. How am I supposed to fit into Colorful Colorado without my colored petals?"

Miss Daffodil looked at Violet.
She had a thought. She reached for a pot of soil
on a tall shelf and handed it to Violet.

"What color do you see?"

Violet looked down at the soil, "Brown, why?"

Miss Daffodil poured paint onto a color palette.
"When you mix yellow and blue, you get…"

"Green," Violet said.

"When you mix blue and red, you get…"

"Purple," Violet said.

"But what happens when you mix red, orange, yellow, green, blue, and purple?" asked Miss Daffodil.

Violet watched the colors swirl back and forth. Slowly but surely, the colors turned to a warm shade of...

"Brown," Violet whispered.

"When you mix your red, orange, yellow, green, blue, and purple on your plate, the same magical thing happens inside of you to create who you are growing to be..."

Before Miss Daffodil could finish, they heard a loud noise coming from the playground.

"Oh no!" cried Miss Rose. "Baby bud, how did you get under there?" A baby bud had climbed under the hole in the fence.

"We would help Miss Rose, but our petals make us too big to climb under." cried Olive and Jade.

Violet walked closer to the fence. She carefully slid her body underneath and sat down next to the baby bud.

"What's wrong bud?" asked Violet.

"I can't catch a green raindrop, and green is my favorite color," whispered the bud.

Violet was quiet for a couple of seconds and took a deep breath.
"The only way to catch the color you want is to wait," Violet said.

"I don't like to wait," sighed the bud.

"Waiting is hard," Violet said. "but when I'm waiting for my colors, I sing a song. Do you want to hear it?"

The bud looked at Violet and nodded.

Violet and the baby bud crawl out from under the fence. "Little bud I was so worried about you," said Miss Rose.

"I'm feeling better," said the bud. "Listen to this song Violet taught me."

"Greens and yellows and reds and blues
These are a few of my favorite hues
One by one they fall from the sky
Find my leaves now don't be shy"

As the bud finished singing, one tiny green raindrop fell from the sky. The baby bud's face lit up with the biggest smile Violet had ever seen.

"It feels good to help someone, doesn't it?"
Miss Daffodil asked.

"All I did was teach him my color song," Violet
said simply.

"To you, it might just be a song, but to
someone else, it's a new way to look at the
world," Miss Daffodil said.

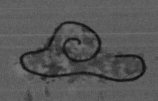

Violet looked down. She grazed the spots
where her petals should be. Why hadn't hers
come yet?

"I want to show you something," said Miss
Daffodil. "Follow me."

Miss Daffodil brought Violet back to the art room. She showed her a picture of a little green bud. It looked just like Violet.

"This was a green bud who also worried about when her petals would come," said Miss Daffodil. "But she was growing in her own ways. She learned to paint, she learned to kind, and most importantly, she learned to try her best."

"You can grow in all kinds of ways. You can paint beautiful pictures. You can teach a baby bud how to wait for his favorite color. Growing isn't always on the outside."

Sunny Daffodil

1985

Violet thought about the flower she was growing to be. She knew the colors on the inside were the ones that counted.

Violet smiled at Miss Daffodil, "I guess I do belong in Colorful Colorado after all."

Meet the Authors

Meet Lauren Goldman and Olivia Cafone—two educators from New Jersey. They sought out to create a text that highlights growth in all its different colors and shapes using springtime and their experience working with growing minds as inspiration.

Lauren is currently a music teacher in Northern New Jersey. She holds a Bachelors of Music in Music Education from Westminster Choir College in Princeton, NJ. Lauren aims to use music and literature to encourage identity growth and creative expression in her students and flowers everywhere.

Olivia is an elementary school teacher who received her Bachelors in Psychology and Masters in Elementary Education at Fairleigh Dickinson University. She is planning a big move from New Jersey to the Colorful Colorado herself in a few months. She believes in fostering students self expression to give them a creative outlet to plant the seeds they need to grow.